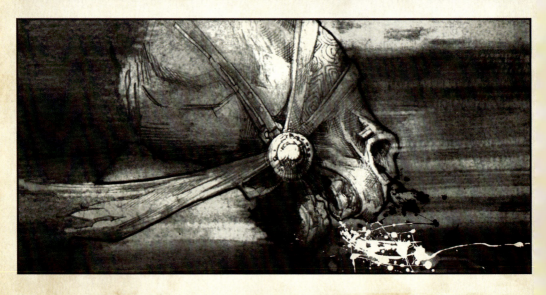

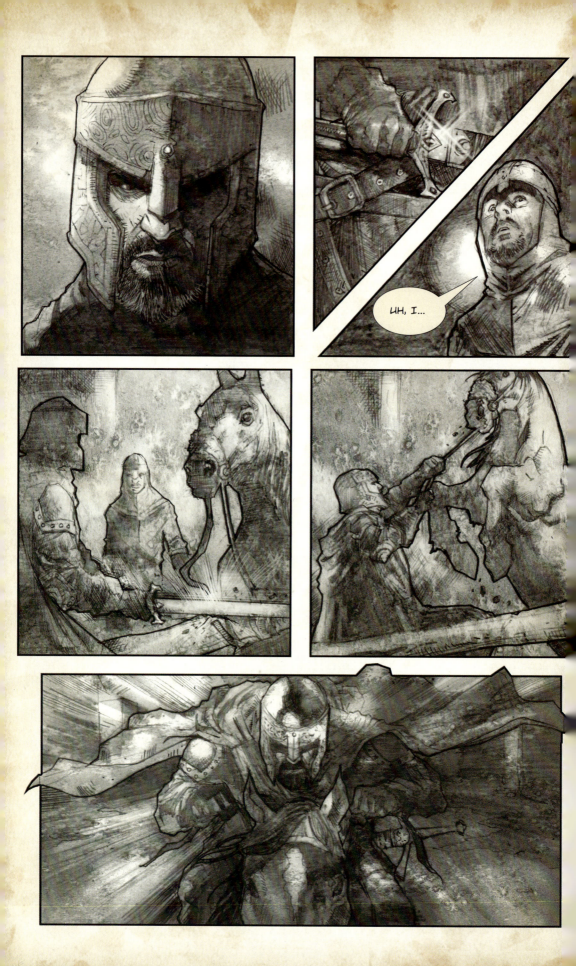

ARE YOU EXPECTED?

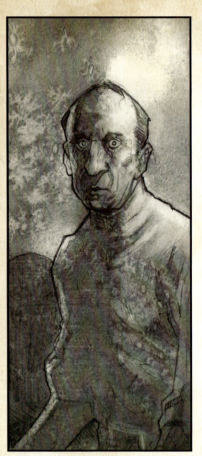
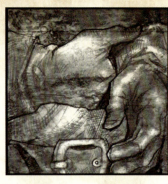

WHAT IS...?

KRNAAGG!!!

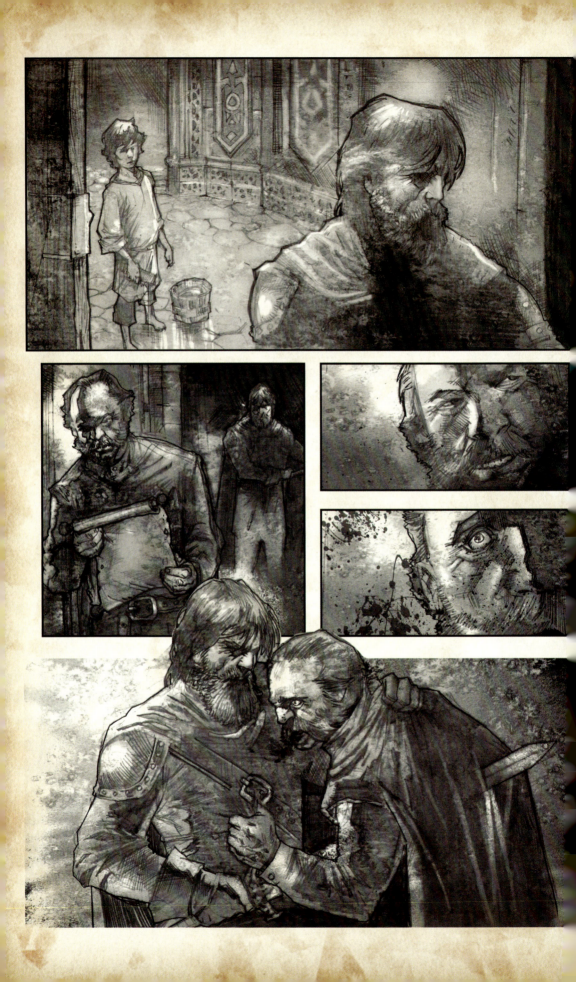

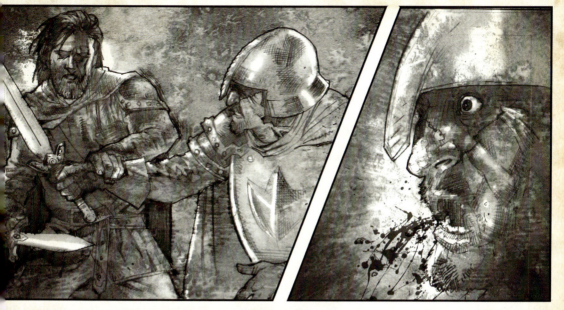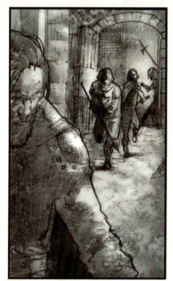

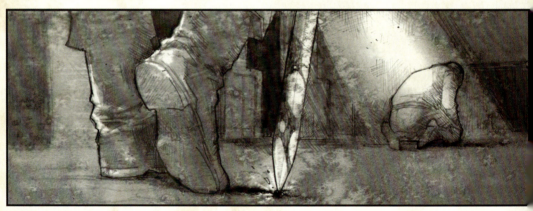

"I KNEW YOU WOULD COME."

THWOOOOP!!!

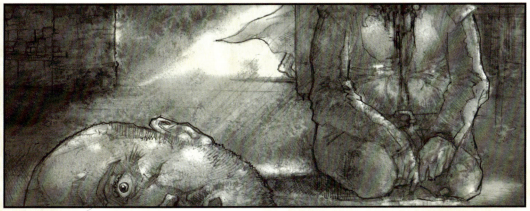

Ice Fang looms tall and ominous, the highest peak in all of Calaway. Some say it is the tooth of a great dormant dragon, and when it awakens, it will swallow the countryside and heavens above.

Three nights in a row the city has sprung to life with torchlight. Packed from wall-to-wall, and still more come each day.

It can only mean one thing....

WAR.

WOULD YOU LIKE TO REST AWHILE, ALYCEA?

NO, THAT'S OKAY.

All rivers lead to *Laden*.

What's that, Alycea?

Nothing. Just a saying back home.

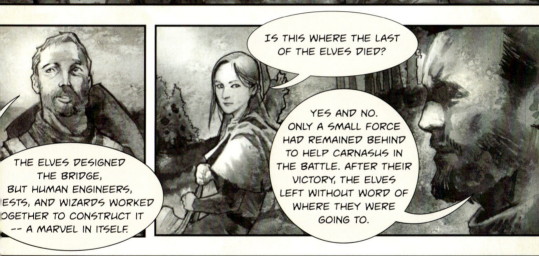

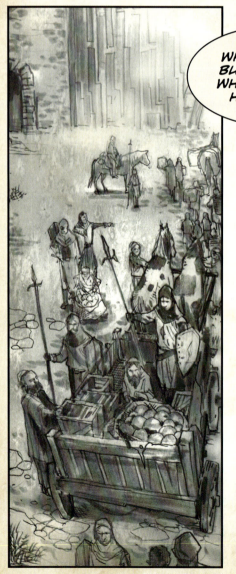

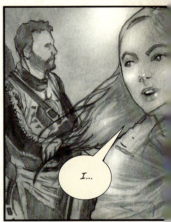

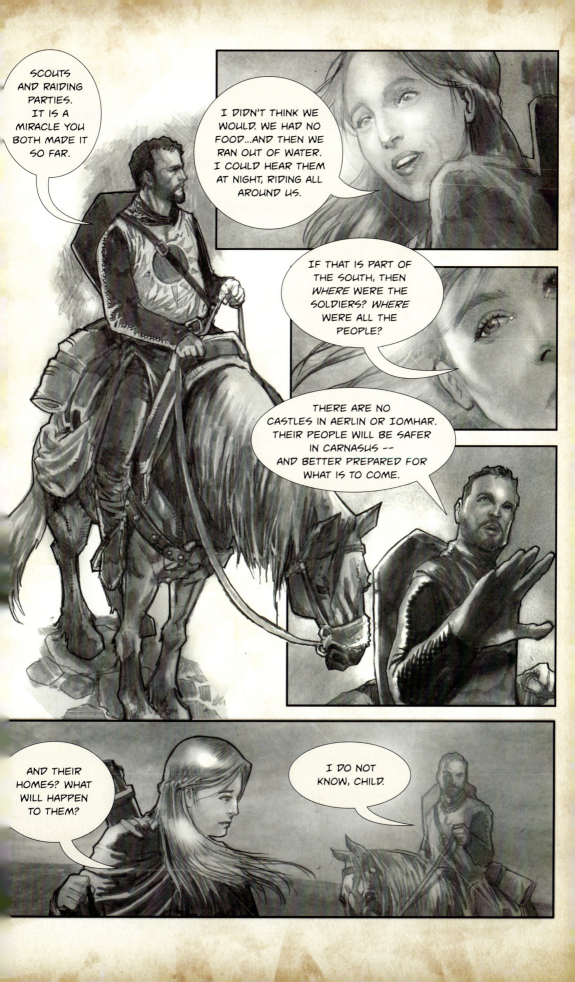

DO YOU SEE THE CLIFFSIDE? MERCHANTS AND FISHERMEN HOOKUP THEIR GOODS TO ROPES TO PULL THEM UP TO THE CITY.

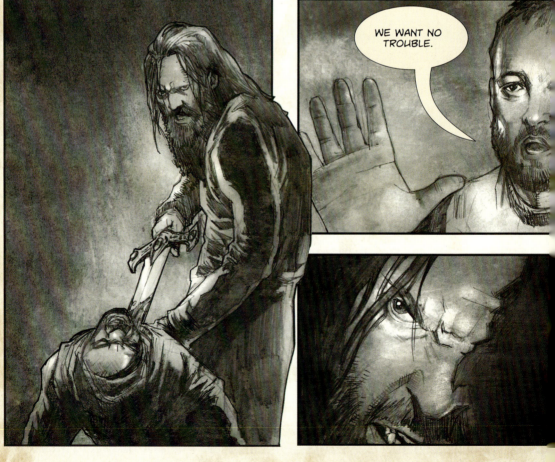

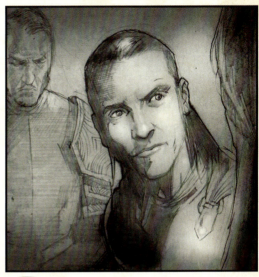

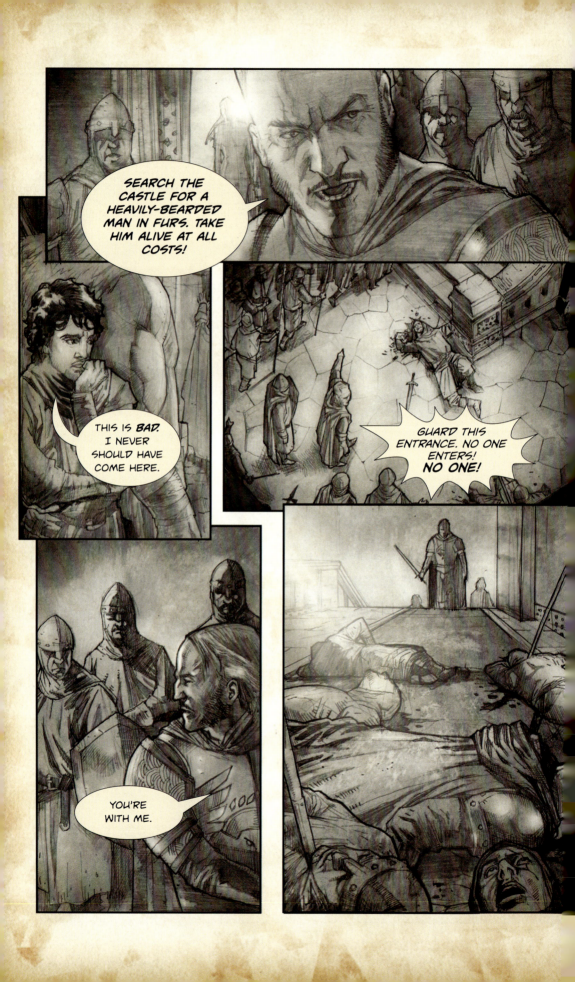

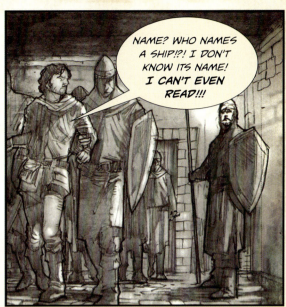

LORD...I...UH, GENERAL....

DIBRI, TELL THE GUARDS AT THE LAST CELL TO REPORT HERE -- I WANT YOU TO RELIEVE THEM.

GUARD, WHEN THEY ARRIVE, TELL THEM TO JOIN THE REST OF THE MEN AT THE END OF THE HALL. NO ONE ENTERS THIS DOOR WITHOUT MY SAY-SO.

MEN, SECURE THE HALLWAY. DIBRI, WAIT INSIDE THE CELL ROOM UNTIL I ARRIVE AND DO NOT SPEAK TO THE PRISONER.

GENERAL, I...

TAKE THIS KEY AND HURRY ALONG. I'M COUNTING ON YOU. **NOW GO!**

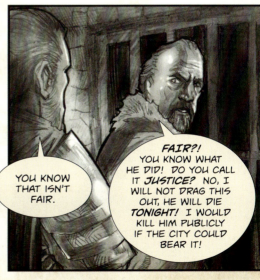

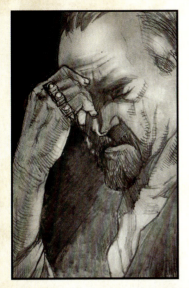

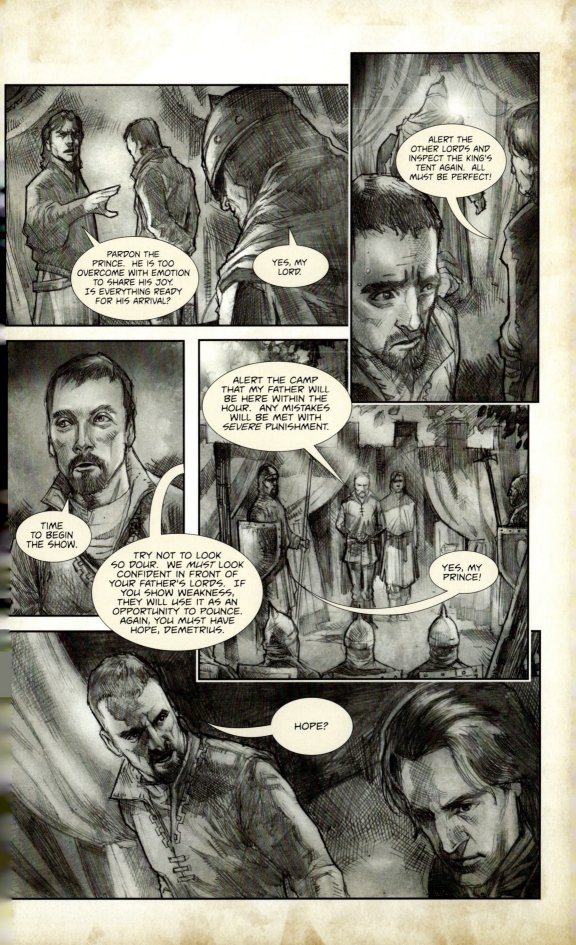